Copyright © 1984 American Greetings Corp. All rights reserved. Published in the United States by Parker Brothers, Division of CPG Products Corp.

Library of Congress Cataloging in Publication Data. Gondosch, Linda. The Strawberryland Choo-Choo. Baby Strawberry Shortcake.
SUMMARY: When all Baby Strawberry's friends want to ride her new tricycle, she thinks of a clever way that they all can share it.
[1.   Bicycles and bicycling—Fiction]  I.   Title
II.   Series.  PZ7.G587St  1984  [E]  83-22085  ISBN 0-910313-24-5
Manufactured in the United States of America   1 2 3 4 5 6 7 8 9 0

# Baby Strawberry Shortcake

# The Strawberryland Choo-Choo

Story by Linda Gondosch
Pictures by Pat Sustendal

BUMP! Baby Raspberry Tart's red wagon bumped into Baby Blueberry Muffin's purple wagon. PLOP. Out they tumbled into Baby Strawberry Shortcake's berry patch. Their eyes popped wide open when they saw Baby Strawberry's shiny new tricycle.

"Do you like it?" asked Baby Strawberry Shortcake.

"I sure do!" said Baby Blueberry Muffin.

Baby Raspberry Tart sighed. "I wish I had a tricycle."

"I was just taking this basket of strawberries to Baby Cherry Cuddler. She has a cold. These will make her feel better."

"Let me take them, Strawberry." called Baby Blueberry Muffin. "I want to ride your tricycle."

Baby Raspberry Tart frowned. "Hey, I'm next."
"OK, Blueberry." said Baby Strawberry
Shortcake. "But be careful."

Baby Blueberry Muffin took the basket of berries and zoomed away. Toot! toot! went the tricycle horn. The pedals spun around and around. She stuck her feet high in the air. "Wheeeee! This is fun!"

She was going so fast that she didn't notice
Baby Lemon Meringue and Frappé Frog. "Help!"
cried Baby Lemon Meringue when she saw Baby
Blueberry Muffin coming. SPLASH! She jumped
into the pond.

THUMP. The tricycle bumped into a stump. The basket of berries flew into the air and fell like strawberry snow. PLOP, PLOP, PLOP. One juicy strawberry landed on Baby Lemon Meringue's head. SPLAT!

"Watch where you're going," Baby Lemon
Meringue cried. "You almost hit me!"

"Oh!" gasped Baby Blueberry Muffin. "I'm so sorry. Here, let me help you." She pulled a dripping Baby Lemon Meringue out of the pond and then pedaled slowly back to Strawberry's berry patch.

"Did Baby Cherry Cuddler like my berries?" asked Strawberry. She looked into the empty basket.

"Not exactly," said Baby Blueberry Muffin.
"I sort of spilled them."
Baby Strawberry Shortcake's mouth flew
open. "Spilled them?"

Baby Blueberry Muffin plopped down next to a mud puddle and began to slap together a juicy mud pie and some little mud muffins.

"Here, Strawberry," said Baby Raspberry Tart. "Let *me* ride your tricycle. I'll zip another basket over to Baby Cherry Cuddler. I promise I won't spill a single one."

Baby Raspberry Tart climbed onto the new tricycle. Her little monkey, Rhubarb, hopped on behind her.

"Don't be gone long," called Baby Strawberry Shortcake. "And tell Baby Cherry Cuddler I hope she feels better."

"I will," called Raspberry. She pushed the pedals of the tricycle. Around and around the berry patch she flew.

"Look at me, Strawberry. I can go really fast! Watch this."

"Be careful!" called Baby Strawberry Shortcake.

Rhubarb jumped up and down, chittering and chattering. "Isn't this fun?" said Baby Raspberry Tart, turning around to see him. She forgot to watch where she was going.

CRASH! Smack into Baby Blueberry Muffin
went Baby Raspberry. GLUMP! Up from the back
of the tricycle shot Rhubarb Monkey, like a
cannonball from a cannon. He sailed through the
air and landed on top of Baby Blueberry
Muffin's head.

Strawberries flew
everywhere and Rhubarb
opened his mouth wide to
catch them as they fell. PLOP.
PLOP. PLOP.

"Ouch! My head!" cried Baby Raspberry Tart.

"My tricycle!" said Baby Strawberry Shortcake.

"Glubmff!" said Baby Blueberry Muffin. She wiped the mud from her face.

"You ought to watch where you're going,
Raspberry. Look what you've done."
"I'm sorry, Blueberry, but maybe *you*
should watch where you're sitting!" said Baby
Raspberry Tart.

Baby Strawberry Shortcake wiped some
mud from her tricycle. "We'll never get my
strawberries to Baby Cherry Cuddler."
Baby Blueberry Muffin hopped back on the
tricycle. "Give me one more chance, Strawberry."

"I'll deliver the berries. I won't spill any." She tooted the horn. She wanted so much to ride the tricycle again.

"Now wait a minute, Blueberry." said Baby
Raspberry Tart. "My turn isn't over yet."
"Yes, it is! Now it's *my* turn to ride."
"I want it!" said Baby Raspbery Tart.
"No! You had it long enough."

"Let me have it, Strawberry." Baby Raspberry
Tart pulled the tricycle away from Baby
Blueberry Muffin.

"You can't have my tricycle, Raspberry." said Baby Strawberry Shortcake.

"Aw, Strawberry!"

"And you can't have it either, Blueberry."

"Why not?" asked Baby Blueberry Muffin. "I'll take good care of it."

Baby Raspberry frowned. "I thought you were my friend, Strawberry."

"But I am your friend. I'm everyone's friend. That's why we will *all* share my tricycle."

"That's impossible," said Baby Raspberry Tart.

"Nothing is impossible." Baby Strawberry Shortcake closed her eyes and thought very hard. "I've got it! Let's make a tricycle train."

Baby Strawberry Shortcake quickly pulled
Baby Blueberry Muffin's purple wagon behind
her tricycle and pushed Baby Raspberry Tart's
red wagon behind the purple wagon.

Then she broke off a curly strawberry vine
and tied the tricycle and wagons together.

"I'll be the engineer," Baby Strawberry called. "You be the conductor, Blueberry. And Raspberry, you be the passenger."

"We have a special delivery to make to Baby Cherry Cuddler." Baby Strawberry Shortcake gathered another basket of ripe, red strawberries and put them onto her tricycle.

"A tricycle train!" said Baby Raspberry Tart.

Baby Blueberry Muffin climbed into her purple wagon. "All aboard the Strawberryland Choo-Choo!" she called. "Watch out for the cow on the tracks."

"That's no cow, silly. That's Custard," said Baby Raspberry. "Hop on, Custard."

Toot, toot, toot went the horn. "Woooooo-Woooooo," sang Baby Blueberry Muffin.

"Chug, chug, chug, chug, chug, chug," said
Baby Raspberry Tart.

Soon all the kids in Strawberryland had joined

the Strawberryland Choo-Choo.

"You're right, Strawberry," said Baby Blueberry Muffin. "We can all share your new tricycle. Is it my turn yet to be the engineer?"

"Everyone gets a turn."

And the wonderful Strawberryland
Choo-Choo went chug, chug, chugging happily
down the path to Baby Cherry Cuddler's garden.